How the Rhino

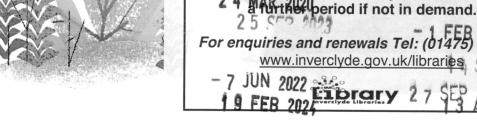

by Rudyard Kipling

Retold by Rosie Dickins

Illustrated by John Joven

Once upon a time, all rhinoceroses had horns on their noses, little piggy eyes and tight, smooth skin.

Their skin fastened underneath with three buttons, just like the buttons on a coat.

One rhinoceros in particular was very big – and very rude.

He had no manners then, and he has no manners now.

One day, this rude rhinoceros
smelled something sweet.
Something tasty. Something
that made him lick his lips.

It was a CAKE!

sugar

currants

plums

The rhinoceros ran at the cake and he spiked that cake on the horn of his nose. Then he galloped away and gobbled it up.

The cake-maker muttered and tutted. "Them that takes cakes makes *dreadful* mistakes!" he said.

And he began to collect the crumbs...

A few weeks later, there was a heatwave.
The sun beat down, and it got hotter
and HOTTER and HOTTER.

The sea looked cool
and blue and inviting.

"Time for a swim,"
thought the rhinoceros.

He waddled into the water,

leaving his skin on the beach.

SPLISH!

SPLOSH!

While the rhinoceros blew bubbles and made water spouts, the man took that skin and he shook that skin, and he filled it with old, dry, crusty cake crumbs.

Then the rhinoceros put his skin back on.

It itched and tickled, from all the crumbs.

Gah!

When the rhinoceros tried to scratch, it itched and tickled even MORE.

He rolled and
rolled, down
sandy dunes.

He rubbed and
rubbed, against
jagged rocks.

He tugged and tugged,
until his skin stre-e-etched.

But whatever he did, those cake
crumbs itched and they tickled.

Then – DISASTER!

Ping!

Ping!

Ping!

He tugged so terribly,
his buttons popped off.

"Oh no," he wailed. "Now I can't take off my skin!"

And *still* those cake crumbs itched
and scratched and tickled him.

From that day to this, the rhinoceros has had baggy, saggy skin and a VERY bad temper — all on account of those crusty, old cake crumbs.

But he never stole a cake again.

How the Rhino got his Skin is from the book
Just So Stories by Rudyard Kipling, which tells stories
of how animals came to be the way they are.

Edited by Susanna Davidson
Designed by Sam Whibley

First published in 2017 by Usborne Publishing Ltd., Usborne House, 83-85 Saffron Hill,
London EC1N 8RT, England. www.usborne.com Copyright © 2017, 2016 Usborne Publishing Ltd.